WILL EARNS HIS MARK

WILL EARNS HIS MARK

BOYDS MILLS PRESS

Published by Boyds Mills Press, Inc.
A Highlights Company
815 Church Street
Honesdale, Pennsylvania 18431
Printed in the United States of America

Publisher Cataloging-in-Publication Data
Main entry under title :
Will earns his mark : and other stories of long ago / compiled by the editors of Highlights for Children.—1st ed.
[96]p. : cm.
Stories originally published in *Highlights for Children*.
Summary : Stories of children living in the eighteenth, nineteenth, and early twentieth centuries.
ISBN 1-56397-448-7
1. Historical fiction—Juvenile literature. [1. Historical fiction.]
I. Highlights for Children. II. Title.
[F] 1996 CIP
Library of Congress Catalog Card Number 94-72489

First edition, 1996
Book designed by Tim Gillner
The text of this book is set in 12-point Garamond.
Distributed by St. Martin's Press

10 9 8 7 6 5 4 3 2 1

CONTENTS

WILL EARNS HIS MARK

By Marilyn Kratz

Will filled the melting kettle with tin and copper for the next day's pewter. Then he came to look over his father's shoulder.

"That's the finest platter you've ever made," said the boy.

"You have said that before, son," Mr. Wickham said, laying his hammer aside. "This time I hope you are right, and I hope General Brighton agrees."

"It's not fair!" Will blurted. "There are other orders ahead of his. But they must wait while you make an entire set of pewter platters for him. How long must we allow the British to order us about?"

"We are English subjects," Mr. Wickham said.

"I'm an American!" Will protested. "Someday soon our country will be independent."

"There is much talk of that lately," said Mr. Wickham. "I wonder if these struggling colonies are truly ready for freedom." Then he turned the large platter over and, using a metal form, placed a crown design on the back.

"Why do you use that English-style mark?" Will asked scornfully.

"I am proud to place that mark on my pewter, for I always make my pieces as fine as I can," said Mr. Wickham sternly. "When you have become a skilled pewterer, you may choose a mark of your own. Now, clean the shop before supper."

"Yes, sir," Will mumbled as his father left the shop. "Someday," Will thought, "I will be a fine pewterer in this new country."

After sweeping the shop, Will gathered the bits of pewter left on the worktable. These he carried to a box at the back of the shop.

"At last I have saved enough scraps to make a porringer for Mother's birthday gift," he said to himself. "I hope I can finish it in time."

The next day, after Mr. Wickham had left the shop, Will melted the scraps of pewter to make the porringer, a shallow silver bowl with handles.

He carefully poured the grayish liquid into a special mold, then he hid the mold under a cupboard.

"Tomorrow I will take the porringer from the mold," he thought as he cleaned the shop.

Will could hardly wait for his father to quit working the next day. But Mr. Wickham worked longer than usual. Finally he said, "Will, we must come back to the shop each evening to work until I finish the platters for General Brighton. You will clean the shop in the mornings before school."

"But, Father . . ." Will began to protest.

"Will!" Mr. Wickham silenced his son. "I know you resent the British. But I have a job to do. We must work extra hours to finish it in time."

"Yes, Father," Will said, wondering how he would ever find time to work on the porringer.

Will couldn't sleep that night. He kept thinking of the hidden pewter. At last he got out of bed. He dressed and went to the pewter shop.

It was cold and dark in the shop. Will quickly lit a candle. He removed the pewter from the mold and began to work.

During the next few weeks, Will made many nighttime trips to the shop to work on the porringer. It was just two days before his mother's birthday when he finally finished it. He polished it until it gleamed. Then he set it on the table and eyed it critically. He had designed its simple, graceful lines. "Is it a good piece?" he wondered.

Will turned the porringer facedown on the table. Using a sharp tool, he etched his mark onto the bottom of it. Then he wrapped it in a soft cloth and placed it far back in the cupboard.

The very next afternoon, General Brighton and another soldier entered the shop.

"Good day, Mr. Wickham," said the general. "How are you progressing with my platters?"

"We have two left to make," said Mr. Wickham. "You may see the platters I have finished."

Mr. Wickham led the two soldiers to the cupboard at the rear of the shop. He took two platters from the cupboard and gave one to each man. Will watched them examine the pewter platters.

"Very good," said the general. "I see your mark is similar to that used by English pewterers. I presume you learned your craft in England."

"Yes, sir," said Mr. Wickham.

Will felt like shouting, "He is an American pewterer!" But he remained silent.

As the general reached into the cupboard to replace the platter, his coat cuff accidentally brushed the cloth of Will's porringer.

"Ah, a porringer," said the general, lifting it out. Will held his breath.

"This design is quite unusual," observed the general. "What a lovely piece of pewter." He turned it over. "The mark is unusual, too."

Mr. Wickham looked at the porringer in surprise.

"Gentlemen," he said with a smile, "this porringer is the work of an American pewterer—my son!"

Now General Brighton looked surprised.

"Well, you colonists are developing some skilled craftsmen," he said. The other man agreed.

After the soldiers had left, Mr. Wickham said, "Will, you have earned the right to your own mark."

"Thank you, Father." Will beamed as he touched the mark he had made on the porringer. "I shall always use this mark—a proud American eagle."

Mary's Vigil

By L.H. Phinney

Mary stood in front of the small log cabin. Her blue eyes were serious as she watched Mr. and Mrs. Smith ride away. They were going to the settlement twenty miles away. She watched them for as long as she could, until their carriage disappeared from sight.

It was just growing light in the east. Clouds hovered low above that stump-dotted clearing in the Vermont forest. The biting wind swung her brown braids and her homespun skirt. A snowflake fell against her cheek.

Mary was a "bound" girl. In exchange for food and a home, she worked for a family. She was "bound out" to Mr. and Mrs. Smith until she was of age. Mary's parents had died, and she had no relatives. For eight years Mary had lived with the Smiths. They were good to her, and she often wished that they were her own parents.

The Smiths had settled in the township of Guilford, Vermont, and were clearing a farm in the wilderness. There wasn't another settler within ten miles. Now Mrs. Smith had a bad tooth, and Mr. Smith must get a few supplies for winter. So they had left fourteen-year-old Mary to look after the children—Benjamin, five years old, and Mercy, three—and the cow in the log barn near the cabin.

As Mary turned back to the cabin, she was remembering Mrs. Smith's parting words. "I know you will take good care of the children, Mary. We shall try to be home tonight, but I trust you completely with looking after the house."

The children woke up. Mary dressed them and prepared the breakfast—cornmeal mush and milk, sweetened with maple syrup. Then they all went to the barn while Mary fed and milked the cow. In those days of open fires, it did not do to leave small children alone.

Snowflakes were falling thicker as they came in from the barn. The ground was white. Mary knew she must get in a good supply of wood. It was cold, and the fire must be kept going. After she got the children involved in building corncob houses, she began to carry in some wood. Then she baked a johnnycake over the fire, using a cast iron pan with a long handle.

They had no clock, only a "noon-mark" on the wall. But this was good only when the sun was shining. So when Mary thought it was nearly night, she took the children to the barn, and fed and milked the cow. When they returned to the cabin, it was snowing, and the wind moaned in the trees.

After supper—more cornmeal mush and the johnnycake—Mary told stories and sang to the children. Then she put them to bed in the low trundle bed that was rolled beneath the large bed in the daytime.

Mary sat by the fire. There was no other light. Candles were used only to read by, or when special work had to be done. The snow was drifting, and the wind whistled about the cabin. Mary knew the Smiths would not be home that night.

Then—what was that? Not the wind! Again, faint and far away . . . then nearer. Mary had heard it in other winters—the call of the wolves!

Her breath came quickly as she listened. She was not afraid for herself or for the children. No wolf could break through a log wall. The windows were small openings with sliding shutters. An oak bar across the heavy door held it securely.

But the low barn had a roof made of hemlock bark. Could the wolves break through that? She thought she heard the moo of the cow mingled with the howling of the wolves, now close about the cabin.

Mr. Smith's gun hung on the wall, but Mary had never fired it. Then she remembered that wolves are afraid of fire!

Quickly Mary grasped the fire tongs and seized a blazing stick from the fireplace. She slid back the window shutter and threw the stick out among the wolves. With howls of fear they fled to the forest, only to come creeping back as the fire died away. Then she threw another burning stick to send them fleeing once again.

All through that long winter night Mary guarded the cow barn and kept the wolves at bay. The children slept. The wind blew. The wolves howled. And when the howls sounded too near the cabin, Mary threw out another burning stick. She was glad she had brought in plenty of wood.

Daylight came at last, and the wolves left. Mary dressed and fed the children. Then they all went to the barn, and Mary took care of the cow.

By noon the storm was over. But Mary had no sleep that day. Always she must watch and care for the children. She dreaded the coming night.

But just as it was growing dark, the Smiths arrived home. They found everything as they had left it, except for the dark circles under Mary's eyes and the burnt sticks that showed black against the snow.

They did not say much. But Mary went to bed that night with Mrs. Smith's words still sounding in her ears: "I knew I could trust you, Mary." She felt proud and happy.

I have often heard my grandmother tell this story. Mary was HER grandmother.

Pioneer Spirit

By Marilyn Kratz

John stripped the kernels from a stalk of wheat and showed them to his father. "Do you think my field is ready to harvest, Pa?" he asked.

Pa bit into a kernel. "It'll hold another two days," he said. "You know Henry Neilson is looking for us to help raise his house tomorrow."

"But I don't want to take a chance on losing my crop!" protested John. "It means seed for next year and a little money to save so I can have a claim of my own someday."

"A twelve-year-old boy has plenty of time before he must worry about such things," said Pa.

"But, Pa! You said working hard to make it on your own is the real pioneer spirit!" argued John.

"That's only part of it," said Pa firmly.

John could see it was no use arguing further.

"Ma's about ready to go," called John's sister, Mary. She came running from the little hillside dugout that was their home. "Won't it be fun to go to a Sunday meeting again, John? I'll see Clara and Christine, and we'll hear a real preacher for a change. I hope he knows some new songs."

John ran to help Ma with the food basket.

"The horses are jittery today," said Pa as he came around in the wagon. "Flies must be bothering them."

"Or the heat," said Ma, pushing ringlets of damp hair off her forehead. "We're all tired of it after so many days without rain."

"It's just the right weather for my—our—wheat," said John.

"I'm glad there's at least one claim shanty up in this region," said Ma as they started for the Linborg homestead. "It is nice to have a proper roof over our heads when the circuit preacher is here."

Several wagons were already standing around the small one-room house when they arrived. After a few minutes spent greeting their neighbors and meeting Reverend Hackett, the morning service began.

John tried not to fidget during the long sermon. At last noon came. Happily, he joined his friends in the shade of a big cottonwood tree to wait until the food baskets were unpacked on long outdoor tables.

"Pa says it's storm weather," said Harold Linborg. "It often storms after such a long, hot spell."

"There's not a cloud in the sky," John said, squinting up at the blue-white brightness.

"But feel how still and heavy the air is," Harold went on. "That's hail and storm weather."

"Come on. Let's get our plates," said John. He didn't like talking about storms when his wheat was so tall and almost ripe.

John could not keep his mind on the service after dinner. His eyes seemed to be drawn to the windows. He could see heat waves shimmering above the dry prairie. There was an oppressive feeling in the hot, still air.

John unbuttoned the top button on his shirt and brushed a fly off his knee. Then he glanced out the window again. What he saw made the hair on the back of his neck stand up.

A long, dark gray cloud was moving in from the west. With each second, it seemed to grow larger and nearer.

John glanced at Pa. He, too, was watching the cloud, a worried look in his eyes. Mr. Linborg and Charley Larson were whispering nervously near the door.

Reverend Hackett paused in his prayer and looked up. He saw the approaching cloud and said calmly, "Perhaps we had better see about the change in the weather."

John hurried outside with the men. A sudden gust of cold wind made his damp shirt feel like ice. In the distance he heard a low rumbling sound coming across the prairie.

"Hail," said Mr. Linborg.

"Pa! My wheat!" cried John.

"We can't beat that storm back to our claim," said Pa.

John fought back angry tears. All those hours of hard work—breaking sod, planting seeds, pulling weeds—he couldn't let them be wiped out in a few minutes of furious weather.

"But we must do something!" John shouted.

"We can save some of the wheat in that field if we cut it down," said Reverend Hackett, pointing to Mr. Linborg's field just beyond the claim shanty.

"Good idea," said Pa, with a determined look on his face. "Come on folks, we will show the storm that it can't have everything!"

The men ran to their wagons to get knives, hatchets, or whatever they had. Then they began to cut Mr. Linborg's wheat as quickly as they could. The women gathered the cut stalks and laid them in bundles with the stems overlapping the kernel-filled heads.

John took his hunting knife from under the wagon seat and ran to the field. He slashed at the wheat, taking out his fury and frustration on the slender, golden stems.

Together, the friends and neighbors worked until the cold, wind-driven rain forced them to return to the claim shanty. They were barely inside when hail began to pound on the wooden roof.

John looked out the window at the large balls of ice bouncing like popcorn on the hard-packed earth of the prairie.

"At least we saved enough for everyone to have seed next spring," said Mr. Linborg.

"Seed for *everyone*?" John asked, surprised.

"Yes, everyone," said Mr. Linborg. "You really deserve some, John. I never saw a boy work with such spirit as you did out there."

"Working together," said Reverend Hackett. "That shows real pioneer spirit."

Tory Hole

By Phyllis M. Hemphill

Jed slowly plodded up the hill to the maple grove. It was hard walking this first day of spring in 1776 because two feet of heavy snow still covered the frozen ground, and the crust had completely softened since morning.

Melting snow from the trees dripped down Jed's neck. He flung off his red knitted scarf and hung it on a branch. The blue skies and warm sun made it seem like spring, but Jed knew winter had by no means ended. It would snow at least three or four times more before mid-April. He quickened his pace because he knew exactly what he was going to do after he finished his chores.

As he neared the first maple tree, he could almost hear it pumping sap. Gathering the sap was simple. Jed's older brother, Giles, had whacked a notch in the maple tree, and another notch an inch below. Into this bottom cut Giles had stuck a broad chip of wood.

Drawing closer, Jed could see the sap trickling down the bark and out to the end of the chip. Then it dripped into the little trough set underneath.

Jed went from tree to tree, checking the troughs in the clump of maples. When a trough was full, he lugged it to the nearest iron kettle and dumped it.

He wondered what Giles was doing with the Committee of Safety in the village. How could he, Jed, a boy of eleven, help his country in its fight for freedom?

Jed remembered well the heated discussion at the supper table last night. His father had been discussing the temporary constitution adopted by New Hampshire in January. Now all of the men in the colony over twenty-one years of age were expected, though not required, to sign a paper supporting independence for this colony. If they didn't, they would be suspected of being Tories. Jed's father said he would be the first to sign. Giles had remained silent. Was Giles a Tory?

His mother, who was usually so quiet, had said that you couldn't judge people by the clothes they wore. There was good and bad on both sides. You had to sit it out.

Jed emptied the last trough, stumbled down the hill, and raced along the dirt road.

Outside the meeting house a throng of men's voices were raised in argument. Jed searched for Giles and found him standing in a corner with three other men. Giles was saying, "I will take no side. I will not sign it."

Jed's mouth fell open. Then it was true! His brother was a Tory! At that moment a hand fell on his shoulder. Jed looked up at his father's bearded face. "Come along home, Jed. I have signed it, and we will fight for our liberty."

"Shall we wait for Giles, Father?"

Jed watched his father's face become dark as a thundercloud, and his words were so low Jed had to strain to hear them. "He did not sign the paper. I will not shelter a Tory."

His father crushed his three-cornered hat on his head and marched out to his horse. He beckoned Jed to mount behind him. It was a long and silent trip home.

That night as Jed lay awake in the loft, a whispered conversation reached his ears.

"I tell you, Martha, Giles was not the only one who didn't sign. Thirty other men refused to sign also. Some refused on moral grounds, opposing the use of force to stop the hostile advances of the British fleet. But many were Tories. If Giles wants to join the Tories, he will not enter this house. No son of mine will be a Tory."

Jed could hear his mother's muffled sobs coming from the other room. Unable to sleep, he crept quietly out of the house.

His boots made a crunchy sound in the quiet moonlit night. Jed breathed in a mouthful of frosty air. Suddenly, the sound of footsteps made him halt. He had reached the clump of pine trees. Now he hid behind one of them.

The shadow of a man's figure moved across the trail and passed a few yards ahead. It looked familiar, although it was laden with a huge backpack. It was Giles, and he was leaving home. Jed had to know where he was going.

Agile as a monkey, Jed climbed a towering pine. By the light of a full moon, he searched the area. A road ran along the Connecticut River and then to a glacial outwash. "It looks like a half mug," thought Jed. "The handle would be the escape ravine, and it looks as if it leads roughly north, up from the hiding place."

A group of uniformed men were gathered around a fire. Jed was about to climb down and warn Giles when he saw Giles emerge from the brush and hand a paper to the leader.

"I can't believe it," groaned Jed when he saw Giles. Was he to lose his older brother? When Jed's baby sister died, he had learned what it was to lose someone.

"No," decided Jed. He would talk with Giles, plead with him to return home.

Spurred on, Jed scrambled down the tree and, in the darkness of the shadowy pines, followed an old trail. His ears alert, Jed was quick to hear a man drinking water from a spring. Grabbing a heavy stick for protection, he raised it as the man turned around.

"Giles," gasped Jed, dropping the stick.

"You followed me," accused his brother.

Jed looked warily around him but didn't answer.

"They're gone," Giles said.

"The Tories, you mean," blurted Jed. "You're one of them!"

Giles was silent. He stared at his brother for a long moment. Then he winced with pain.

"Jed, you've grown older this winter. And taller. I think I can trust you with a secret. Come sit here beside me." Jed sat down and watched Giles remove his boot.

"Your ankle is swollen," said Jed in surprise.

Giles grunted. "I twisted it. But no matter. I want you to do something for me. I want you to remember that it's not always easy to tell the truth. It's even harder to keep a secret. Can you keep a secret?"

Jed nodded, his eyes wide with surprise.

"Take off your boot."

Jed did as directed.

Giles reached into the toe of his boot, withdrew a piece of oilskin-wrapped paper, and placed it in the toe of his brother's boot. "You see, Jed, I'm known as a Tory to our friends, but I can often bring valuable information to the American officers. I go from one camp to the other taking letters. I want you to cross the Connecticut River and give this message for General Washington to the artillery officer. Remember, give it to no one else."

"Trust me, Giles. I will go with all speed, and your secret is safe with me," said Jed. He grinned down at his brother, who was risking his life as a spy. Then his face sobered. "Couldn't we let Father and Mother know the truth about you? Mother wept all night."

Giles nodded. "But no one else," he said firmly.

Deep inside Jed there was a wonderful feeling of contentment. He called back, "I'll see you in time for maple sugaring."

Cathy and the Wolves

By Mildred Bair Lissfelt

In 1812 there lived in a log cabin in Westmoreland County, Pennsylvania, a little girl named Cathy who liked to ride horseback. Sometimes she rode Star, the older and slower of her father's two horses, through the woods to the country store. But this did not happen often because most of her family's food and clothing were raised or made right on their own farm. One day her father broke his axhead while chopping wood and asked Cathy to hurry to the store for a new one.

"I can't hurry on old Star," Cathy complained. "Please, please, Father, let me ride King."

"King is a grown-up's horse," her father said, with a scowl on his face.

"But you said I can ride Star as well as anyone," Cathy reminded. "I heard you tell Mother. And I am sure I can ride King, too."

Her father laughed and rumpled the yellow curls on her head.

"Very well," he said. "But be careful with him. Horses are hard to come by in this country."

One of her brothers helped Cathy mount the big black horse, and the whole family watched her ride across the little bridge at the edge of the clearing. Cathy was sure she could ride King well, but she would not be satisfied until her father thought so, too.

Once out of sight of the farm, Cathy wanted to make King run. But then she remembered her father's warning to be careful, and decided it was better to let him walk. Even at a walk she could make better time than with Star, who was fat and lazy as well as old. And, by walking, King did not frighten away the birds in the trees or the squirrels and rabbits along the road. There were many of these small forest creatures, and all seemed to be enjoying life as much as Cathy.

Since her father was in a hurry, Cathy did not dismount when she reached the store. She simply called to the storekeeper, who was standing in his doorway, and told him what she wanted. He brought it to her in brown paper, twisted at the end so that she could hold it easily.

"Be careful with it," the storekeeper said. "It is the very last one I have."

"Why does everybody tell me to be careful?" Cathy thought after she had thanked the storekeeper and started home through the woods. "First Father tells me to be careful with King, and now the storekeeper tells me to be careful with the axhead. Of course I shall be careful."

And she was careful—balancing the axhead in front of her with one hand and holding tightly to King's reins with the other.

As she rode along, she began to feel that something was wrong in the woods. There were no birds rustling or chirping in the trees, and not a single squirrel or rabbit scampered along the road. Something had frightened the small woods creatures and must be lurking nearby. Cathy was sure of this when King began to shy off to one side.

"What is it?" Cathy wondered, urging King on with a slap of the reins. "Is it a bear or a panther or a wolf?"

Of all the larger animals in the forest, Cathy feared the wolves most. She had been told they ran in packs and seldom came near people in daytime. Yet their howls on many a night outside the log cabin had sent chills through her. What would it be like to meet a wolf face-to-face?

As if in answer to her question, a great gray animal—somewhat like a dog, but larger and thinner —sprang out of the woods with a snarl and leapt up at her. King, who had been twitching nervously, sensed the danger before it was upon them. With head down, he bolted through the woods at a gallop. Away went the axhead wrapped in brown paper. Cathy had all she could do to hang on. But hang on she did, twisting her fingers in the long black hair of King's mane and holding on tightly. It was no longer a question of walk or run, but of how fast the horse could go and whether he could outdistance the ferocious wolf and the pack she was certain was not far off.

"Hurry, King, hurry," Cathy urged, feeling the threat of wolves closing in. "Faster, faster!"

But King was already running as fast as he could, with the road home seeming longer than ever before.

"If only we can get past the bridge," Cathy thought. "The wolves will not dare to cross the bridge into the clearing."

She looked back again, and there were four wolves at King's heels, jumping up but just missing horse and rider. She looked ahead and there, at long last, was the bridge.

"Hurry, King, hurry," Cathy urged again.

They reached the bridge and King thundered across it, making all the planks rattle. Cathy, looking behind again, expected to find that the wolves had given up the chase. But they followed, crossing the bridge right after them.

"Father, Father," Cathy screamed as King raced toward the farm buildings.

Now there were shouts and more shouts. Father, Mother, and Cathy's brothers and sisters came running from all sides, picking up sticks or stones or anything else handy. By the time King came to a trembling stop at the barn, the wolves had slunk off into the woods. Cathy slid off the horse's back and ran into her father's arms.

"Oh, Father, Father, I'm so sorry."

"It's all right, honey," her father said, stroking her hair. "It was no fault of yours that the wolves came here."

"I—I'm not upset because of the wolves," Cathy sobbed. "I'm crying because I couldn't be careful. I let King run too fast, and I lost the axhead."

For a brief moment everybody was silent. Then Cathy's father spoke.

"But you were careful, Cathy. As careful as any one of us could have been. You were careful to hang on tightly and keep your head and get home safely. No one could have done more than that."

"But the axhead, Father. It was the very last one in the store."

"Don't you worry about that," her father said. "The wolves don't want it, and we'll be sure to find it after the pack has run off to the hills."

He lifted her chin with his finger and smiled down at her.

"You were a brave girl, Cathy. Mighty brave. And I, for one, think you ride King better than any of us."

Settlers on the Delaware

By Jean H. Mitchell

Jim Lowell was nearly twelve years old when his family joined a dozen or more other families to resettle along the banks of the Delaware River. It was a long and tedious journey from the Connecticut town where they lived. The ox-drawn wagons were piled high with supplies and precious possessions, and everyone except the very youngest children had to take turns walking.

The days that followed their arrival seemed almost like a dream. There were days of hard work before they could move from the wagons to their small one-room log cabins—all pretty much alike, with dirt floors, a mud-and-stone fireplace, and one window to let in sunlight and air. Jim's father placed their cabin on high ground near a good spring, for he knew full well that in the springtime an ice jam in the river could easily flood the valley and cause great hardship.

Winter came with its snow and freezing chill. Time had been too short to plant all the necessary herbs and vegetables for food on the floodland along the river. The rich river deposit would yield many good crops next summer, but there was the question of survival until spring, with the threat of piercing winter storms.

There were also rumors of foraging tribes. The settlement constructed a fort from logs about twelve feet long, which they hewed on four sides with a broadax. A high place on the bank was selected with a good view up and down the river. The logs were set on end about three feet into the ground for support. Inside, a well was dug and a shelter made for the women and children.

Jim now became his father's right-hand man. Often, with an old muzzle-loader and his dog, Skip, he crossed and recrossed the frozen river and climbed the mountains on both sides. He was happy when he could bring back rabbits, partridge, grouse, and an occasional deer or bear.

One bitterly cold day when Jim was tracking down a deer near a narrow gorge where the river flowed between two rock formations, he spotted a cave. It would be a good place to rest and get out of the cold, he thought; so with Skip at his heels he headed for the cave. As he rounded a boulder, he came face-to-face with a Delaware Indian boy. They stared at each other. The hair on Skip's back stood straight up as he growled at the stranger. Jim's half-frozen fingers were still in his mittens—not on the trigger of his gun. The other boy's tomahawk lay on a rock near a small fire. Except for the wind in the nearby pines, all was still.

Suddenly, the Delaware Indian boy reached out his hand toward Jim. Jim, taking off his mitten, held out his hand. That handclasp was to be remembered for a long time afterward.

"Come," the boy said, gesturing for Jim to follow him into a cave. The cave was surprisingly warm. The boys sat and talked with few words and many gestures for what seemed a long time. Jim could hardly keep his eyes off the tomahawk on the rock nearby. The head and handle were of expert craftsmanship, and the wooden handle was inlaid with eagle feathers.

Dark had already fallen when Jim reached home. His father and mother had begun to worry, for they knew very well the dangers he might encounter. They were relieved when he appeared, and were surprised and pleased when he told about his newfound friend.

At last winter was nearly over. The ice in the river had broken up, and great chunks were floating downriver or piling up along the banks. The sap had started to run in the hardwood maple trees. It was time to make the syrup and the sugar for the year.

Jim was hunting deer, for the family was badly in need of meat. As he worked his way along the river, he saw a buck on the bank just ahead. Instantly the muzzle-loader came to Jim's shoulder. But as his finger pulled the trigger, his foot slipped in the snow. The buck jumped and slipped onto an ice floe at the river's edge. Quickly Jim slid down to the ice on the bank. But as he was reloading his gun, the ice broke loose from the shore.

The ice floe, with Jim on it, swung out into the river. He knew that he was in very grave trouble. Not far down the river was an eddy of swirling water and rocks that would surely smash the ice on which he was slowly drifting. He was far below the cabins and knew there was no chance for help from the settlement. The only sound was the low rumble of the deep water and, in the distance, the roar and crash of the rapids. Suddenly Jim saw someone running far up on the bank, then the figure was sliding down toward the river. As the bushes parted at the bank, Jim saw his friend.

Quickly the Delaware Indian boy uncoiled a rawhide rope from his belt and tied one end to the tomahawk. He planted his feet firmly in the snow and hurled the tomahawk out toward the ice floe. It hit the ice within a foot of Jim. Quickly Jim bent over and grasped it.

Now began the difficult feat of maneuvering among the ice floes to the bank with only a slender rawhide rope between Jim and safety. His friend walked carefully along the bank, placing each foot so that just an even amount of strain was on the rope. Gradually the ice on which Jim stood eased toward the bank—just above the rapids! He jumped ashore and held out his hand to his friend, who was recoiling his rope. The handclasp between them spoke more than words could express.

That evening Jim's family had a most welcome guest for supper, and thus began a friendship which was to mean much to this tiny group of settlers and their Delaware Indian neighbors.

The Day the Bell Rang

By Richard E. Albert

Enoch had just gone to the brook to get a bucket of water when he heard the bell. He stood for a moment, listening. Though it was far away, the sound was clear and mellow, echoing across the countryside. Setting his bucket on the ground, Enoch turned abruptly and stepped over a log that spanned the narrow stream. Then he ran toward the field where his father was working.

"Father," he shouted, "the bell in the State House is ringing."

His father had heard it, too, and, turning away from his plow, looked in the direction of the town lying in the distance along the banks of the Delaware River.

"Do you think it's the celebration the man was talking about?" Enoch asked his father.

"Could be," his father said.

Enoch remembered the man who had stopped by the farm four days ago, saying that important people were meeting in the State House and what they were doing could bring great changes in the land. He had heard there might be a celebration.

"What will it be about?" Enoch had asked when the man was gone.

"Don't know exactly," his father had said. "Maybe something to do with what happened in Massachusetts last year."

Enoch had heard about places like Boston, Lexington, and Concord, but they were so distant. He and his parents went into town so seldom it was hard to know if these things really did happen.

"Can we go?" he now asked eagerly, thinking of all the people who would soon be gathered in the square on this July morning and of the excitement of being there.

"Don't have the time," his father replied crisply. "Late getting the crops in as it is."

Though disappointed, Enoch knew how necessary it was to get the crops in on time.

"Could I go myself?" Enoch asked suddenly. He realized it was a great distance, but it would be worth the nearly five-mile walk to find out what the celebration was all about.

"Well now, Enoch, I don't know," his father answered slowly, pondering the request. "But if you're willing to try, I can't see any reason why you shouldn't. Be sure to start back in time so you'll get home before dark."

Setting out on the road, Enoch was excited but still wondering about what the man had told his father, and about the important people meeting in the State House. They had come, his father was told, not only from Massachusetts but from other distant places, like Virginia and New York. It would have taken them many days riding in a coach with swift horses to reach Philadelphia.

As he drew near the town, he saw pillars of smoke rising in the air, and, in a moment of fright, he wondered if the town were burning and the bell had been ringing to warn the people of the fire.

He started running but, entering the street leading to the square, saw the smoke was from many bonfires. Seeing the throng around the State House, Enoch knew the bonfires, too, must be part of the celebration.

As he moved through the crowd, even the thrill of being there seemed almost like a dream. There were men and women and children—tiny ones being carried in the arms of their parents, some older ones gazing in wonder as he was, and boys his own age making the most of the celebration.

Enoch thought of joining them, hoping they would let him take part in their fun—perhaps, too, learning more about this wonderful thing they were celebrating. But he was so awe-stricken he only watched.

Drawing back to the edge of the crowd, he was remembering the last time he was here, many months ago, before last winter's snow. It was hard to believe there could be so many people even in the entire colony.

As he was standing there, he saw three men approaching. They stopped for a moment to talk. One, an elderly gentleman, turned and, seeing Enoch standing alone, left his friends and walked over to the boy's side.

"You seem to be wondering what this is all about," he said.

Enoch nodded silently, astounded to find that this man knew exactly what he was thinking. The gentleman had a kindly face with little wrinkles around his eyes when he smiled, long graying hair that dropped in back to his collar, and glasses with small square lenses.

"This is indeed a great time, lad," he said.

"But what are all these people doing?" Enoch asked, now eager to find out. "And why did the great bell in the State House ring, and why are all the bonfires burning?"

"Perhaps you don't know it," the elderly gentleman said, "but you'll be living in a new country from now on."

A new country? How could it be? The road he traveled into town, the streets, the State House were all the same as they had been those few times when he had been here with his father. His own home on the farm, the field his father plowed, the brook that ran by the house—no different from what they had always been. There were the same green trees in this early part of summer, the birds singing in the branches, the same bright flowers, and the same sunny days.

What did the man mean by a new country? How could it be, when it was exactly the same as it had been for as long as he could remember?

"I don't understand, sir," he said, very puzzled. "Won't I be living in Pennsylvania anymore?"

"You will still be living in Pennsylvania," the man replied, "though it will no longer be a colony but a state, part of a new nation. Four days ago a document was adopted in the State House. It was called a Declaration of Independence."

"What will this new nation be called?" Enoch asked the elderly gentleman.

The two other men had finished talking and they turned to find their companion.

"Are you coming, Mr. Franklin?" one of them asked, seeing him with the boy.

"I'll be with you shortly," said the elderly man as he turned to Enoch, a twinkle lighting up his eyes behind the square-rimmed glasses.

"The new nation, lad," he said finally, "will be called the United States of America."

The Contraption

By Edith M. Gaines

It was Colleen's turn to grind the corn. She screwed up her freckled face and groaned, "Do I have to, Mom?"

Of course she had to. But ten-year-old Colleen sometimes pouted. There were so many *have-to's* for her and her six brothers and sisters. Her father and mother worked from dawn till dark tending crops in the field next to their one-room log cabin in the Cuyahoga River Valley. All the children had to help with the work. That was the way families lived in the Western Reserve in 1809.

Colleen had a turn carrying water, and a turn milking the cow, and a turn chopping wood. She didn't mind chopping wood, and she liked milking Amanda, the cow. It was fun to watch the milk squirt into the pail. It was fun listening to the steady zing-zing of the milk against the side of the pail. And, best of all, there was a big mug of fresh milk for her to drink when she was finished.

But Colleen did not like to grind the corn. It was too much work. She had to carry the heavy sack of grain all the way down the path to the Masons' clearing. She started out slowly the morning of her grinding turn. Once she stopped to watch two gray squirrels chasing each other up a big oak tree. Once she put down the heavy sack and picked raspberries. Colleen ate a handful, then she picked up her sack and walked on.

Now she could see the Masons' cabin. In front of it was a big stump, and near the stump was a sapling. Colleen stopped when she got to the stump. She let her grain sack slide to the ground. Then she slumped down next to it as if she were too tired to move another step. She lay there resting until she heard her name called.

"Colleen, what are you doing?"

Colleen rolled over and sat up. She saw a tall boy standing in the doorway of the Masons' cabin.

"Hello, Ned. I'm just resting," said Colleen. "I came to grind corn."

"Better get busy," said Ned, "unless you want me to grind first."

Slowly, Colleen got up. She looked over at the big stump. Then she looked at her sack of corn and shrugged her shoulders. "Won't ever get done if I don't start," she said to herself.

She poured the corn into the hollow of the stump. Then she pulled the top of the sapling down and tied it to a stone.

Next, Colleen dropped the stone on her corn. The sapling, on the rebound, lifted the stone a few inches, then dropped on the corn again. This time Colleen had to lift the stone herself and drop it. Each time the stone fell on the kernels, they broke into smaller pieces.

Colleen worked hard, picking up the heavy stone and dropping it again and again. She did not notice an old man walking up the path into the clearing behind her. The man stood for several minutes watching Colleen. Then he said, "That looks like a mighty slow way to grind corn. Don't you get tired?"

"Sure do," agreed Colleen.

"Seems as if there's an easier way," said the man. "In Pennsylvania I've seen mills for grinding wheat. I've a notion to make a little mill that would turn by hand."

Colleen looked at the stranger. He was tall, with white curly hair.

"That sounds like a good idea, Mister," said Colleen. "Did you just come from Pennsylvania?"

"Just lately," replied the stranger. "My name's George Peake. I'm building a cabin by the river."

"I wish you would make a mill, Mr. Peake," said Colleen with a look of hope on her face.

Colleen took a metal scoop out of her sack, filled the sack with the coarse grain, and slung the sack over her shoulder. "I've finished," she called to Ned as she started down the path toward home.

A few weeks later, Colleen's father made a trip to town. When he returned, he said to Colleen, "Looks like you'll have an easier way to grind corn now. In town, they're talking about a new kind of hand mill made by a fellow who just moved here from Pennsylvania."

"That's Mr. Peake," said Colleen. "He has a cabin by the river. I saw him last time I was at the Masons'. He said there was an easier way to grind corn. Where is his hand mill? Can I really use it to grind our corn?"

"You certainly can. Peake's invited all the neighbors to use it."

That was one time Colleen could hardly wait till the day came for grinding corn. She was up early, and the sack of grain didn't seem as heavy.

She paid no attention to the squirrels this time, but hurried straight down the path until she came to the new cabin by the river.

Mr. Peake himself came to the door. "Hello there, young lady. Didn't I see you grinding corn down at Masons' one day? I suppose you'd like to try my contraption."

Colleen nodded. Mr. Peake showed her two flat round stones set in a hollowed-out log. One stone rested on top of the other one and had a hole in the middle.

"Pour some grain into this hole," Mr. Peake said.

Colleen poured. Mr. Peake picked up a stick and shoved it into a small hole near the edge of the top stone. Using the stick as a handle, he turned the stone slowly. Soon a little ground meal spilled out from between the stones.

"Now you try it," Mr. Peake suggested.

Colleen took hold of the stick and pushed the stone around and around. The kernels of corn made a crunching sound as they were crushed between the two stones. It was fun watching the meal spill out into the hollow log. The job was finished in a much shorter time than when she used the sapling and stone at the Masons'.

"Well, what do you think of it?" asked Mr. Peake.

"It's first-rate," said Colleen. "Thanks for letting me use it." She picked up her ground grain and hurried home to tell her family about the contraption.

From that day on, grinding corn was Colleen's favorite job. She liked it even better than milking Amanda, the cow.

The Half-a-Chance Lad

By Bethea verDorn

"I've come about the cook's job," John told the gray-haired man in the ranch office.

The man looked up and cleared his throat. "You saw my sign?"

"Aye. It said, *Cook wanted for shepherd. See Mr. Griggs at Blackstone Ranch. Leaving town June 1,1928.* That's tomorrow." John had counted the days until he could get to the ranch. "Are you Mr. Griggs?" John asked.

"I am. And who might you be?"

"My name's John Mackie, sir. My pa and I came over from Scotland."

"Been in Montana long?"

"Almost six months. Getting settled so we can send for Ma and my little sisters," John said.

Mr. Griggs glanced at John's blackened hands. "You work in the mine?" he asked.

John slipped his hands into his pockets. "Aye, loading coal with my pa." John hesitated. Should he tell Mr. Griggs how much he hated the coal dust and the damp chill of the coal mine? "But I'm looking for a change," he said simply.

Mr. Griggs frowned. "Son, this is a man's job. Mighty lonely grazing sheep. Long days, hard work—but quiet. Not much excitement for a lad like you."

John made himself as tall as he could and looked straight at Mr. Griggs. "I am not afraid of hard work. I don't mind the quiet. And I can cook," he said. "Just give me half a chance."

The shepherd smiled. "I like you, son. You don't waste words." Then he paused. "The job is still open, and it might as well be yours. If your father approves of your working in the fields, report here tomorrow. We load at dawn."

John's father approved, but not without a warning. "Don't go wrong, laddie. Lose this job, and you'll have no job at all. Then there won't be money to send for your ma and the little girls."

"Aye, Pa, I know." John raced to pack the few clothes he owned. Tomorrow he would be on his way to the mountains!

The next day at dawn, the sheep were loaded into cattle cars for the journey west. By noon the train had climbed into the towering Rocky Mountains. It stopped at a small station, where John's first chore was to fetch Bruce, the saddle pony.

"Meet me and the herd at the clearing two miles up the tracks," Mr. Griggs called to him from the caboose. The train pulled out.

Bruce was waiting in the corral, loaded with a pack saddle full of camp gear. The stationmaster greeted John with a doubtful gaze. "I didn't expect a boy," he said. "Think you can handle Bruce? He's a feisty one."

"Aye, I can handle him." John led the pony out of the corral and began the long walk up the tracks. Halfway there, he stopped. "Bruce, how about a wee rest?"

Bruce snorted and kicked a hind leg. "Now don't you be feisty, Bruce. What's the matter?"

John stroked the pony's neck, but Bruce was jumpy. He pawed at the ground and pranced in circles. John held the rope tight to keep Bruce under control. Then, from the tracks behind them, he heard a rumbling noise.

"So *that's* why you're feisty. Don't worry, I won't let any trains run over us." He led the nervous pony away from the tracks and into the woods further away from the sound of the train.

The noise grew louder. Bruce grew more and more agitated. There was a deafening roar, then a thick cloud of dust appeared. This was no train! John's heart pounded, and he gripped Bruce's rope. Fifty or more wild horses thundered past by the tracks.

Suddenly Bruce bolted. The rope burned John's gloved hands as the excited pony dragged him through the woods. "Whoa, Bruce! Slow down!"

John's clothes were badly ripped by snapping underbrush. His bare arms stung with scratches. His shoulders ached. How much longer could he hold on?

He slammed against a tree. The rope lurched painfully out of his grasp, and Bruce galloped off. John lay gasping for breath. His father's warning pounded in his ears: *Don't go wrong, John, or you'll have no job at all.*

Staggering to his feet, he was still doubled over from the blow. If only he could run away like the pony, so he wouldn't have to face Mr. Griggs. How could he explain losing Bruce and all of the camping gear? His only chance was to find the pony. His family's future depended on it.

"I'll find you, Bruce!" John said to himself.

Half a mile down the tracks, John spotted the pony. He could make out the pack saddle on Bruce's back. "Sneak up on him. Don't spook him again," John told himself. He stepped ahead cautiously, tie by tie.

That's when he saw it. First the smoke, then the black engine of a train heading right for Bruce. But Bruce wasn't moving.

"Run, Bruce, run!" John yelled. He raced down the tracks toward the pony as the train approached from the opposite direction. "Get out of the way!" he shouted.

Bruce didn't move. Now John saw why. The pony's rope was wedged tight between a tie and the rail. Bruce *couldn't* move.

The train whistle blared. Panic flashed in the pony's eyes. John grabbed the taut rope and pulled, but his weakened arms couldn't free it. How could he get Bruce off the tracks?

The pack saddle! John rummaged through it wildly. There had to be a knife with the cooking gear. He found the knife, pulled it out, and slashed through the rope. Just as the train barrelled down upon them, he yanked Bruce away from the tracks. The train roared past.

Panting, John glared at Bruce. "Feisty or no, this time you're coming with me!"

The sun was setting when they finally arrived at the clearing. "Been waiting for you, lad!" Mr. Griggs shouted. He stared at John's torn clothing and battered arms. "What happened? Looks as if wild horses ran over you."

"You could say that." John smiled. No need for explanations. He was out of the coal mine for good. He had taken on a man's job. And now he knew that he could do it, given half a chance.

Betsy Stays Home

By Thelma Fick Hunt

Betsy quickly brushed away a tear as she tucked her baby brother in his crib for an afternoon nap. Then she closed the door softly and went back to the big kitchen, where she was about to bake bread.

"How silly I am to cry," said Betsy to herself. "After all I'm twelve and the oldest, too. Naturally I was the one to stay home with the baby!" And she popped the big puffy loaves of bread into the red brick oven.

"You're a young lady now," Mama had said when she and Papa had left this morning. "I know I can trust you."

"Of course she can," thought Betsy, wondering whether she should work on finishing her quilt patches or mending some woolen socks. At that moment Betsy heard a familiar noise. She ran through the house to the front parlor, pulled back the shutters, and looked out. Since the Revolutionary War had ended, many soldiers had passed on their way to the Carolinas. Some stopped to ask for lodging or food. Mama's very last words had been: "Be kind, but firm, Betsy. Tell any stranger who may stop to continue on to the next farm. I don't want strangers in my house while I'm gone."

As Betsy watched out the front window, a large white horse galloped up. A dusty-looking soldier rode on it. "Oh, dear," thought Betsy sadly, "I wish he wouldn't stop, for I will have to turn him away." But already the stranger had dismounted and tied his horse's reins to the white gatepost. "He looks like a gentleman," decided Betsy, watching him closely as he neared the door. The man was very tall, and his dusty uniform was well-made and covered with much gold braid. He had removed his hat before he climbed the porch steps, and Betsy noticed that his hair was white.

Betsy opened the door at his first knock.

The man smiled at her and bowed from the waist.

"Good day, little maid," he said. "Whom have I the honor of addressing?"

"I'm Betsy Brandon, sir," said Betsy, curtsying.

"Well, Betsy, I have been traveling since daybreak. Might I beg a little bread and meat?"

"Oh, no, sir. Not today. You'll have to ride on to the next farm. It isn't far."

Suddenly the soldier looked tired and sad.

"Oh, sir, it isn't that I am inhospitable. It's just that I'm all alone—that is—except for my baby brother. He's in my care," stated Betsy proudly. "But you see, I promised Mama not to let any strangers into the house. Mama, Papa, and the rest of the family went to Salisbury this morning for the celebration."

"Celebration?" inquired the stranger.

"Yes, sir, General Washington is going to be there today." Betsy sighed deeply. "I do wish I could see him. But if you hurry, sir, you might be able to get there in time to see him."

"Yes, I really should get to Salisbury this afternoon," admitted the soldier thoughtfully. "But I'm too hungry to ride that far without some food."

Suddenly the fragrance of the baking bread reached Betsy's nose. "Oh, dear, oh, dear me," said Betsy, puckering her brow. Then she smiled and clapped her hands.

"Oh, sir, I know what I'll do. I won't let you in the house because I made a promise to my mother. But look—look yonder under that tree. If you'll sit down and wait a moment, I'll bring you some fresh bread." Betsy hurried back to the warm kitchen to remove the golden baked loaves of bread. In no time at all she was out on the lawn with plates of warm sliced bread, ham, strawberry jam, and fresh milk.

"This is indeed a treat," said the man emphatically. "Did you bake this bread, Betsy?"

"Yes, sir," replied Betsy.

"You're a mighty good cook, Betsy. This bread tastes as good as Mrs. Washington's."

"Oh, have you been to Mount Vernon?" asked Betsy in surprise.

"Why, yes, Betsy, I've lived most of my life at Mount Vernon." As the stranger said this, he arose and smiled at Betsy.

Betsy stood and looked at him unbelievingly.

The man's smile became a grin. "I'm afraid you don't believe me, Betsy."

Betsy looked puzzled.

"You can't mean that, sir, because if you did, you would be—but of course you're not!"

"But Betsy, I am—I live at Mount Vernon. And now you won't have to go to Salisbury. But *I* do—in fact, I must hurry, or I will not get there in time."

"You mean, sir, that you—you—are—General Washington?" she asked.

The soldier nodded. "Yes, Betsy, I am."

Betsy felt her cheeks going red, "I am very sorry, sir," she said, casting her eyes down in great embarrassment.

"Why, Betsy, aren't you glad to meet me?" the General asked.

"I'm so very, very happy, General Washington. But what will Mama say when she hears I made you eat outdoors?"

"Your mother will be proud of you, Betsy, my dear, because you obeyed her. Always obey your mother. I always obeyed mine."

The General reached into his saddlebag and took out a small silver button.

"Thank you, Betsy, for your kindness," he said, placing the button in her hand.

Before she realized it he was in his saddle and was galloping up the dusty road toward Salisbury. Then she looked down at the small button she held. In the center, beautifully engraved, were the initials G.W.

Josh

By Mary R. Waters

Josh walked briskly, hopping from one frozen mound of dirt to the next, dodging the puddles of slushy snow. He pushed open the heavy oak door of a small brick house. "Good evening, Mrs. Tooke," he said to his landlady, who was kneeling in front of the fireplace arranging a log with a long poker.

"Good evening, Josh. Mr. Kent has not come in yet. We'll wait supper for him," she answered.

Mr. Kent was Mrs. Tooke's other boarder. Although Josh was only fifteen years old, his father had made a contract and apprenticed him to William Gray, a merchant in Boston. Josh was to serve as Mr. Gray's clerk until he was twenty-one years of age.

This was the custom of the times. The country was young. Thomas Jefferson was President, and Paul Revere and his family lived within a ten-minute walk of Mrs. Tooke's house. It was 1803.

After Josh removed his hat and boots, he took a book from his jacket pocket and stood near the window, holding the book close to one of the small panes to catch the fading light. It was too dark to read anywhere else in this room, which, in addition to the glow from the fire, was lit by only a single candle on the trestle table. Mrs. Tooke could not afford to use many candles.

Josh was deep in *Robinson Crusoe,* one of the few books he had brought with him from his home in a town twenty miles south of Boston.

When Josh saw Mr. Kent approaching, he read on quickly. Robinson Crusoe was being battered by twenty-foot waves as he tried to make the shore. Who would be saved in that shipwreck? When Josh had to close the book for supper, he knew he could read no more that night.

After supper, Josh climbed the steep steps to his room at the back of the house. How he wished he had candles and a fire to read by in his room. But Mrs. Tooke did not permit candles to be used for reading after supper, and there was no fireplace in his room. The only way to keep warm was to get under all the bed covers. *Robinson Crusoe* would have to wait until daylight and Josh's half-hour lunchtime tomorrow. After kneeling to say his prayers, Josh climbed into bed and pulled the covers over his head.

Robinson Crusoe was the last of the books he had brought from his home. He had read all the others, and what would he read when that was finished? He could not afford to buy books out of his very small wages.

The next Sunday was cold and windy, and a gray sky threatened snow. Still, Josh followed his custom of taking a walk on Sunday afternoon to explore different parts of the city. On his way back to Mrs. Tooke's through a narrow back street, he paused in front of a store window, a spot where he had lingered many times. The sign over the door read Hastings, Etheridge & Bliss's Bookstore. As wet snowflakes began to whiten his hat and shoulders, Josh cupped his hands over his eyes to peer inside. The store was closed, of course, because it was Sunday, but Josh could see an elderly man stoking the stove inside. Every shelf was crammed with books, and the shelves reached from floor to ceiling.

The man looked up and stared at Josh for half a minute. He closed the stove door and walked toward the window with a slight smile on his face. Then he stepped to the door, opened it, and said, "Would you like to come in out of the cold?"

"Oh, no, sir. I am not going to buy any books," Josh said.

"Never mind about that, lad. Come inside here where it's warm."

Josh stepped through the door. He was damp and cold and very curious to see the inside of the shop.

"I have seen you looking through that window several times. What is your name? I'm James Bliss."

"My name is Joshua Bates. Are these books all yours, Mr. Bliss?" Josh asked as he picked up a copy of *Gulliver's Travels*.

"Well, I do sometimes sell some of them. If you'd like to read that, Josh, sit by the fire and stay for a while. I live upstairs. I'll be back in a half hour."

Josh read for a half hour and prepared to leave.

"Thank you very much, sir. I really enjoyed this book. Unfortunately, I do not have any more books of my own—that is, none I haven't already read."

Mr. Bliss invited him to come back the following Sunday. Thus began a friendship for Josh. By the time spring came, Josh would go to Mr. Bliss's for an hour or so after supper two or three times a week. Sometimes they would talk, and sometimes they would sit on opposite sides of the table, each buried in a book. Once in a while Mr. Bliss's daughter-in-law would visit and make a pot of tea on the stove for the three of them. Josh had found a home away from home.

Prairie Valentine

By Ethel Bretches

Chris Adams pulled his younger sister along the wagon trail. He squinted at the threatening sky, then down at Nell who stumbled along behind him. He slowed a bit but pleaded, "Hurry up, Nell. The storm's closer, and we're still a mile from home."

Through stiff, cold lips, Nell mumbled, "I can't go any faster."

When this February blizzard swept across the Kansas prairie, Miss Bailey, who was the teacher at the one-room school, dismissed her twenty pupils. She knew they had to walk from two to four miles to reach home. She urged them, "Hurry home as fast as you can before the storm gets here."

Twelve-year-old Chris knew sudden blizzards sometimes caught settlers miles from home. He knew that people had been lost just a few yards from their own homes because they couldn't see through the thick, swirling snow. Fear and responsibility for Nell's life and his own squeezed at him.

Maybe Nell could hurry if he got her mind on something else. There was the question of their mother's valentine gift. He asked, "Did you think of something we could give Mama today?"

Nell usually let her older brother, Chris, make decisions. Now she looked expectantly at him and answered, "No. I guessed you would think of something. You always do."

Sometimes Chris resented the responsibilities thrust upon him as the young son of a settler family. He wished Nell would solve some of her own problems. Now the danger of the storm was most important, but maybe he could still think of a gift.

Hurrying along, Chris remembered other times when they had to "make do," as their mother put it. For her birthday last fall, Chris had found some colorful pheasant feathers to trim her winter hat. Just before Christmas their father had brought home two muskrats from traps along the creek bank. With his help, Chris and Nell had made their mother a warm muff out of the skins. But now he couldn't think of anything for her valentine.

Chris thought of the hard life on the prairie. Women had to work all of the time at one task or another. Too much was demanded of boys his age. He had to chop wood; feed their one cow, two horses, and the pigs; and help out with all of the other chores on the farm. Though he had grown taller, stronger, and more sure of himself, he knew he had changed from a carefree boy since his family moved to the Kansas Territory.

It had been different back in Connecticut. Boys and girls played games. Large houses were close to neighbors, and stores were only a few blocks away. Out here their log-and-sod cabin had one large room, a small bedroom, and a shedlike pantry attached to the kitchen. There was only one small square window covered with oiled paper set in the long log wall of the large room. Their nearest neighbors lived more than two miles across the prairie.

When the family's meager supplies ran low, Mr. Adams hitched the team of horses to the big wagon and drove sixteen miles to Benning, the nearest town. The trip took most of a day and wasn't done often.

The sudden sting of icy snow hitting his face brought Chris back to the present. He knew that in a few minutes a fierce blizzard would prevent them from seeing more than a few feet around them.

"Come on, Nell. We've got to run!" He yanked her forward.

Nell—cold, breathless, and getting tired—was ready to blame Chris for their troubles. When he pulled her, she jerked back and flared at him. "I can't. You know these overshoes are too clumsy for me to run in them."

But run and stumble they did until they saw the little cabin not far ahead. Chris strained to keep it in view as snowflakes fell faster and thicker. He tripped and fell, pulling Nell down with him. Feeling a rough hump jabbing his ribs, he realized he was off the wagon trail. Fear of being lost made him weak, but he couldn't let Nell know.

He pushed himself up, started to lift Nell, and then heard a faint squealing sound.

Nell felt something squirming and thrashing beneath her. Terrified, she shrieked and yelled, "Get me up from here, Chris. There's something under me!"

As Chris raised her up, his other hand darted down and grasped a snow-covered, struggling creature. Brushing the snow from it, he discovered a cottontail rabbit. He saw a shallow nest where the rabbit had burrowed under a thick clump of dry buffalo grass for shelter from the storm. But what should they do with it? Should they take it home? Chris needed one hand to help Nell, but could he hold the frightened rabbit with only one hand? There was one way, maybe. He shoved the rabbit into his coat pocket and held it there while he held on to Nell.

"Come on, Nell. We're not far from home now. Let's run."

Excitement made Nell's overshoes light and swift, and within a few minutes they opened the cabin door.

Mrs. Adams threw her arms around them. "I've been nearly frantic," she cried. "Where've you been? Didn't Miss Bailey know the storm was coming?" She tugged off Nell's wet coat while Chris turned away, having difficulty removing his snowy garment.

He pulled his arms out of the sleeves while he kept the squirming rabbit in his coat pocket. Grinning at Nell, he asked, "We found the answer to our problem, didn't we?"

Nell looked puzzled, then, with a giggle, she said, "Oh, Mama, we didn't have a valentine for you. Then we fell down in the snow—right on top of the funniest valentine anyone ever saw. Give it to her, Chris."

The quivering cottontail kicked and tried to get free as Chris held it toward his mother. "It may not be what you want or need, but I guess it's a real prairie valentine."

Mrs. Adams took the animal, put it in a small wooden box, and patted it gently to calm it. She laughed and said, "Well, this is certainly an unexpected valentine. And I think it's the best one I ever had. Thank you both for such a fine gift."

Chris felt happiness spreading through him as he watched his mother soothe the rabbit. "We'll keep it until the snow stops," she said, "and then set it free by the woods."

He grinned and thought how nice it truly was to live out here; how life could be exciting and fun where real, live prairie valentines might be found on a cold winter day.

Polly's Corn Bread

By Joan Strauss

Polly usually did everything fast and not very carefully. When her brother, John, saw her measuring the cornmeal very slowly, he teased, "Watch out! You'll spill it!"

"You don't bother me," Polly said. "This is going to be the very best corn bread I ever made. It's for Father."

"How are you going to get it to him? He is at Valley Forge with General Washington's army. It's half a day's trip from here."

"You don't know everything, even if you are older," Polly said. "Mother and I are going to visit Aunt Martha tomorrow. She lives so close to Valley Forge we can go to see Father."

"Maybe you will even see General Washington," said John enviously. "I wish I could go, too, but I have to stay and take care of the farm. I guess that's what Father meant when he said it's not always easy to be the man of the house."

"I'll tell him how hard you are working on the farm while he is in General Washington's army," Polly promised.

She measured out milk and broke the eggs she had gathered herself. She was just stirring in the eggs when Father's friend, Mr. Hansen, stopped to see them.

"Mrs. Hansen tells me you are going visiting out near Valley Forge tomorrow," he said.

"Yes," replied Polly's mother. "Polly is baking some corn bread to take to her father."

"I wonder if you could take something else with you," Mr. Hansen said.

"I will take what I can," Polly's mother answered. "There won't be much room. We are taking food and my husband's warm winter clothing."

"It's only a message," said Mr. Hansen, "but a very important one for our men there. The British army has settled in Germantown for the winter. They send out so many patrols we have a hard time getting messages to General Washington. We have been waiting for someone we can trust, and someone the British would not suspect."

"Of course we will carry the message," said Polly's mother. "We will be proud to help."

Mr. Hansen warned, "You may be stopped and your belongings searched. Can you think of a good place to hide the message?"

"I will carry it in my shoe, or perhaps sew it into the hem of my gown," Polly's mother decided.

"No, the British are on to those tricks," Mr. Hansen said.

Polly was about to pour her batter into the baking pan. "I will bake it into the corn bread," she said. "The British will never find it there. Only Father will."

"A fine idea, little maid. Into the corn bread it goes." Mr. Hansen handed Polly a small piece of folded paper.

"Won't the writing be spoiled by the baking?" asked John.

"It is written in good India ink. It will stay," said Mr. Hansen.

Now Polly had a double reason for making sure her corn bread baked just right. She was very careful. When the bread had cooled, it was packed with other things for their morning's journey.

Polly did not think of the message again until she and her mother were riding through the countryside. Horses' hooves sounded from a side road. A British patrol caught up with them even before they could see the red-coated soldiers through the trees. A British soldier said they had orders to search every traveler.

One of the soldiers smiled at Polly from his tall horse. "I have a little girl just your age at home in England. She made this for me before I left." He pulled a kerchief from his pocket and showed Polly the white-and-yellow daisy embroidered on it. "Can you do that?"

Polly shook her head. "I can make corn bread, though." She was too anxious to say more because the other men were going through their boxes and baskets. She could not help an "Oh!" as they almost overturned the hamper with the corn bread.

"Be more careful there!" ordered the soldier who had spoken to Polly. "Did you bake that?" he asked when one of the men lifted the napkin covering the corn bread. "If so, I would like to have a piece. Will you let me see if the American ladies bake as well as the English ladies?"

He was nice. Polly liked the twinkle in his eye. The corn bread was the best she had ever made. She would like to show him that even if she could not embroider daisies, she could bake good bread. But suppose he bit into the piece with the message? Somehow, she must not let him have her corn bread.

"No!" she yelled at him, pretending to be upset. "It's not for you! It's for my father! Nobody else can have any!" She picked up the basket and clutched it to her.

"I apologize for my daughter's manners." Polly had never seen her mother so dignified. "The soldiers frightened her. May we go on?"

"Yes, of course." The soldier on the tall horse bowed. Polly's mother bowed back and picked up the reins. She began to give Polly a scolding, which lasted until they were out of sight and hearing of the British patrol.

"You may put the hamper down now, Polly," she said. "You were a brave girl. You saved the message. I am sorry that I had to give you such a scolding, but it was for the British soldiers to hear. Your father will be eating that corn bread for his supper tonight."

But he never did. He sent the corn bread with its important message straight to General Washington's headquarters.

"Don't feel sorry I didn't taste the corn bread," he told Polly. "I will when I come home. With young women like you to help us defend our freedom, we will all come home soon."

I'll Manage

By Marilyn Kratz

"Look at all the people, Pa," said Thomas. "Do you reckon that they're all expecting something on the riverboat?"

"People naturally flock to town when there's a boat due," said Pa as he guided the horses and wagon through the crowded street.

"I don't see the boat," said Thomas, looking toward the river.

"It'll be along soon," said Pa. "Can you manage the horses while I find out exactly what time it will arrive?"

"Me, Pa?" Thomas hesitated. Pa had never before allowed him to handle the horses in town. He sat as tall as he could on the wagon seat. "Sure, Pa. I'll manage."

Thomas held the reins tightly as his father walked toward a group of men on the dock. The horses pranced nervously as other wagons hurried by, but Thomas held them steady.

In a few minutes Pa returned, looking troubled.

"The boat won't arrive until midafternoon," he said. "I can't spend an idle day waiting in town when there's so much to be done on the homestead before winter sets in."

"But we can't leave without that load of lumber we ordered for the house," said Thomas.

"I know," said Pa. "Your ma doesn't want to spend the winter in our hillside dugout." He looked up at Thomas, who was still holding the nervous horses steady. "Thomas, I wonder . . ."

Thomas knew what Pa was thinking.

"Do you figure—maybe—I might bring the lumber home?" he asked.

Pa did not reply. Instead, he said, "Wait here," and hurried to the men on the dock. After a brief conversation with them, he ran back to the wagon.

"Sam Fletcher will give me a ride home. It's on his way," Pa said. "Mr. Hawkins and his boys will help you to get the lumber from the boat onto the wagon." He put a small leather pouch into

Thomas's hand. "Here's money to pay for the lumber and to buy yourself something to eat at noon. Try to get home before dark."

"Yes, Pa." Thomas stuffed the pouch deep into his pocket. "I'll manage."

In a minute Pa was gone. Thomas was alone in town for the first time in his life. He took a deep breath and said again to himself, "I'll manage," and he hoped he would.

The day passed quickly as Thomas watched the activities along the river. When the boat came into sight at last, the riverfront swirled with excitement.

Thomas checked the horses. Then he joined Mr. Hawkins on the dock.

Several people got off the boat before the cargo was unloaded. One of them, a tall man wearing the white collar and black coat of a clergyman, approached the men near Thomas.

"Good day, gentlemen," he said. "I'm Pastor Philip Sawyer. Could you tell me where I can find Mr. Jason Hawkins?"

Thomas saw Mr. Hawkins's mouth open in surprise. "I'm Hawkins," he said. "But we didn't expect you until next spring. We have not built the church yet."

"Oh, that's quite all right," Pastor Sawyer said cheerfully. "We can hold services in the schoolhouse until the church is built."

"But we have no school either," said another man.

"Then we shall have to establish one," the young man went on, smiling confidently. "I am qualified as a teacher as well as a minister. Now then, any building will do. Perhaps a hotel or store."

"The hotel is always filled with homesteaders, coming or going, and the stores are open for business every day," said one of the men.

"A home, then?" Pastor Sawyer asked hopefully.

The men exchanged uncomfortable glances. Thomas knew most of them lived in small dugout homes, as his family did.

Pastor Sawyer looked from one man to another. The confident look faded from his face. He cleared his throat and said quietly, "Perhaps I'd better not stay."

"Oh, please stay!" Thomas blurted. "Ma is always saying how much she misses going to church, and my sisters and I have never gone to school. Please stay! You may use our lumber for a building."

Thomas stopped suddenly when he realized what he had said. He stepped back and looked down, embarrassed at having spoken so boldly.

It was very quiet for a minute. Then Mr. Hawkins spoke. "My boys need schooling, Pastor. I, too, will donate my load of lumber for the building if you'll stay."

"I've no lumber, but I'll help build," said another.

"Wonderful!" Pastor Sawyer's face beamed again. "I'll get my bags. Then I'll help unload lumber."

Thomas' heart seemed to beat in his throat as he helped unload the lumber. He thought of the house Ma wanted so much, and he remembered promising Pa he would manage to get the lumber home safely. What would they say when he told them he'd given it away?

"Thomas! What kept you?" Pa called as Thomas drove up to his home that evening. "Where is all of the lumber?"

Ma and Thomas's sisters came out of the dugout.

"I'm sorry, Ma," Thomas began. It was difficult to speak with such a tight feeling in his throat.

"Come inside, son," said Ma. "Tell us about it while you eat."

But Thomas was not hungry. He gulped down a cup of water. Then he told exactly what had happened in town. "It seemed the right thing to do," he finished. "Was it, Pa?"

Pa looked at Ma. She smiled.

"Yes, son," said Pa. "Our lumber will do more good for more people in a school and a church."

"We have a snug place to spend the winter," added Ma. "I'm proud of you, Thomas."

"I'll go to town tomorrow to help raise the building. We will need to get it done before snow flies," said Pa. "I know you can manage things around here while I'm gone, son."

"Now do you think you can eat your supper?" Ma asked, smiling.

Thomas laughed, a feeling of relief sweeping over him. "Yes, Ma," he said happily. "I know I can manage that!"

Mile-a-Minute Millar

By Peggy Cameron King

In 1847, the Millar family had moved from Scotland to Canada. Martha was seven then. Now she was nine and looking forward to the most thrilling adventure of her life.

Martha needed help to carry out her plans, or she would not have confided in her sister, Elizabeth. Elizabeth was two years older than Martha. But she was a cautious person, so the whole idea scared her.

"I don't think you should do it, Martha," Elizabeth protested. "Only government officials and the railroad directors are supposed to be on this trial run. Besides, think of the danger! Have you forgotten that while they were building the roadbed, one engine jumped the track and was almost lost in the swamp?"

"Father and his men slaved for two years to build the eight miles of track between Montreal and Lachine. I think his family should be allowed to share the day of triumph," Martha insisted.

"'Tis a great day for Father and for Canada, to be sure," Elizabeth admitted. "Mother will be called to the platform when the speeches begin. There'll be a band, too. But you and I are supposed to take care of the twins."

"You can manage alone, sis. That's when I'll slip into the train," Martha planned. "There will be so much excitement that no one will notice. Father will be making history. And if this test is successful, the company will begin to build railroads all across Canada."

"Steam locomotives are too dangerous. They will never replace stagecoaches or steamboats." Elizabeth spoke with such timidity that Martha was irritated.

"Nonsense!" she said. "Don't let Father hear you talk like that. Everything new isn't dangerous. The day will come when travel by train will be common. I wouldn't be surprised if someday there would be flying machines, too."

"Don't be silly," said Elizabeth. She didn't approve of Martha's daring plan, but she was too loyal to refuse her help.

On the afternoon of the great day, the station platform was crowded with excited spectators and with the important persons who were to board the train for the trial run. When Martha's mother was called to join Superintendent Millar on the platform, Martha slipped quietly away from her sister and the twins and boarded the last of the three passenger coaches. She crouched down behind a rear seat. She was uncomfortably cramped, and the dense smoke that billowed in from the woodburning engine made her eyes smart. She heard her father's voice boom, "All aboard!"

The officials entered and nervously spread out their coattails as they seated themselves on the hard seats. They all wore tall black stovepipe hats because this was such an important occasion. Their voices were loud and excited.

"If this line is a success, gentlemen, we can put our horses out to pasture."

"I tell you the railroad is here to stay."

"I hope that foolhardy Sandy Millar won't go too fast on the curves. He insists on being at the throttle for this initial run."

"Hang on, gentlemen. We're off!"

The train gained momentum. In less than a minute its occupants found themselves jouncing and bouncing in every direction. Suddenly an extra lurch hurled Martha from her hiding place into the aisle. There was no use trying to remain hidden. She grasped the arm of a seat and held on.

None of the men paid any attention to the stowaway. They were too busy trying to keep upright, grasping their hats and grabbing for each other or any support they could get hold of. Their voices became louder and their tempers flared as the train sped along the track at a terrifying rate.

"Mark my words, we'll jump the track! Hang on!"

"I'm a mass of bruises, and I canna see!"

"Sandy Millar must be daft. We'll all be killed!"

Suddenly tall Mr. Molson shot upward. His hat was crushed and pleated against the ceiling. Mr. Molson lost both his dignity and his temper. "I'm as beaten as me hat. Will we never get there? If I set a safe foot on land, you'll never get me in one of these contraptions again."

The breakneck speed of the train lessened as it approached Lachine. The shaken and frightened men tried to regain their composure. A little more than eight minutes had passed since the train had left Montreal.

As the train halted, there was a mad scramble as the distressed passengers rushed to get out. Somehow Martha got to her feet and followed. Her Sunday-best clothes were torn and soiled, and she ached all over.

Big Sandy Millar jumped down from the train cab and faced the crowd of passengers and spectators assembled on the platform. His voice rang with excitement and pride. "We made it, gentlemen! A speed record—eight miles in eight minutes!"

Before the sorely tried officials could comment, a cheer rose from the thrilled crowd that had assembled to await the arrival of the train. Women and children waved banners and flags. Bagpipes shrilled an additional welcome.

Mr. Molson's worried expression slowly gave way to one of mingled wonder and pride. He shouted and waved aloft his crushed hat.

His fellow officials likewise forgot their discomforts and joined in a cheer. "Hurrah for Sandy Millar! Three cheers for the Flying Scotsman!"

Young Martha's heart swelled with excitement and pride. How happy she was that she had shared this milestone in transportation history!

That evening Martha showed her sister her bruised shins and the lump on her head. "Didn't I tell you the railroad is here to stay?" she bragged. "You won't find any horses that can go sixty miles an hour. I'm sore and stiff, but I wouldn't have missed it! I can't wait to tell my grandchildren! Just imagine, I'm a Mile-a-Minute Millar!"